Proud

This book is dedicated to:
The inspiration and pride of my life – my family. – Fred
My family ✖, friends ⼍, and Chuck P. – Vickey

Text copyright © 1997 by Fred Penner
Based on the song "Proud" lyrics and music by Fred Penner © Branch Group Music Publishing
Illustrations copyright © 1997 by Vickey Bolling

Whitecap Books,
Vancouver/Toronto

Produced by Vickey Bolling
The text of this book is set in 48 point Kidstuff. The illustrations are in acrylics,
dyes, gouache, and pastel on handmade oriental paper.

1st Softcover Printing, 2001
Canadian Cataloguing in Publication Data
Penner, Fred.
Proud
ISBN 1-55110-650-7 (bound). -- ISBN 1-55285-274-1 (pbk.)
I. Bolling, Vickey, II. Title.
PS8581.E5538P76 1997   jC813'.54   C97-910385-1
PZ7.P3847Pr 1997

The publisher acknowledges the support of the Canada Council and the Cultural Services Branch of the Government of British Columbia in making this publication possible. We acknowledge the financial support of the Government of Canada through the Book Publishing Industry Development Program for our publishing activities.

Printed in Hong Kong, China

PROUD

written by Fred Penner
drawings by Vickey Bolling

You've got to be proud of the people around you;

Proud of the
things you do.

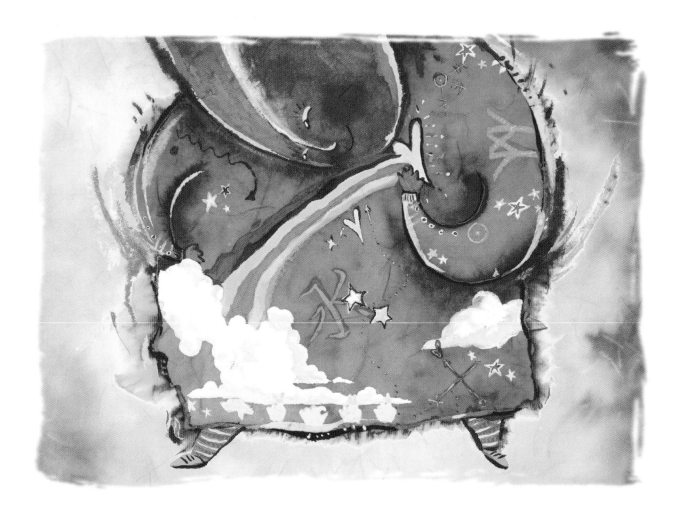

Proud of your dreams
and your feelings inside:

Have the courage to
let them shine through—

Have the courage to make them come true!

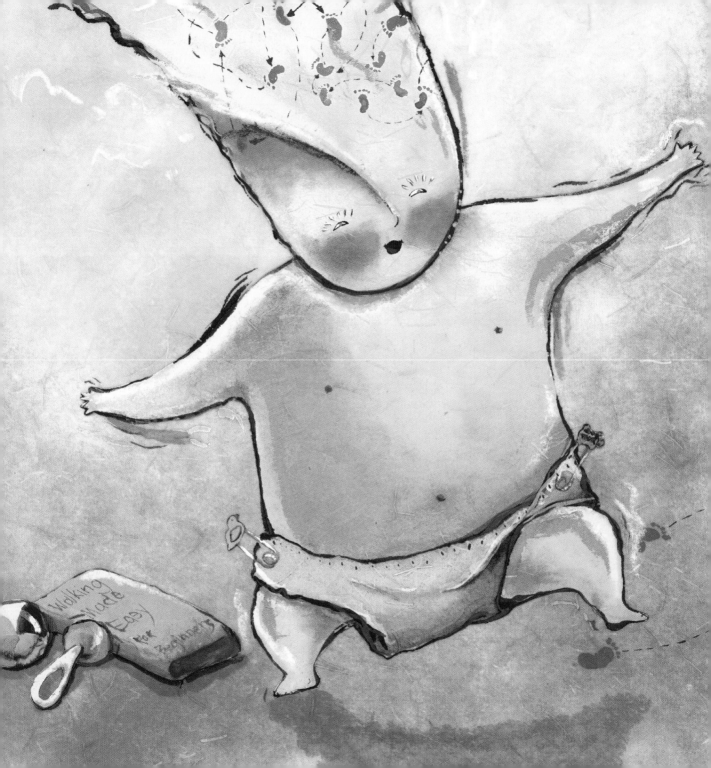

Look at the children
learning to walk.

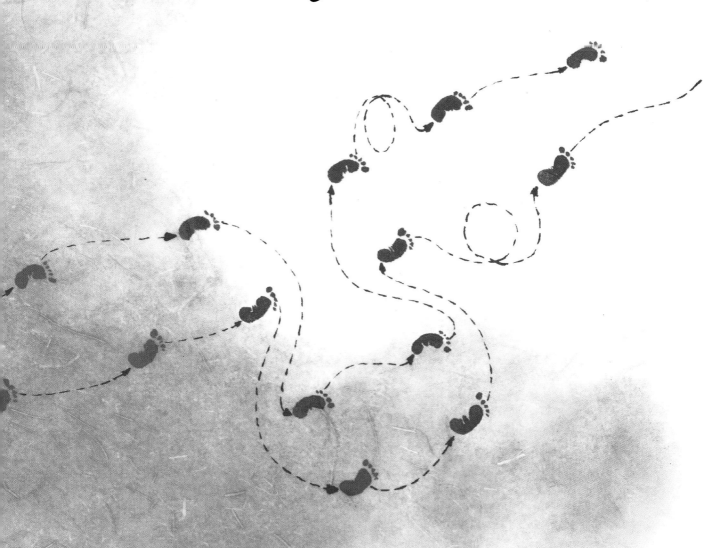

Hear the wonderful sounds . . .

. . . as they're learning to talk.

Finding something new
each day.
There's only one thing
you can say . . .

Orange Juice
GET A BOOST
FROM OUR JUICE

Reciting a rhyme,

Helping a friend through
a difficult time.

Is the perfect place to start.

When you know that you did
the best that you could,

The end of your journey
will make you feel good.

The faces of parents
at their baby's birth,

Glow with a pride
that's the greatest
on earth!

Proud

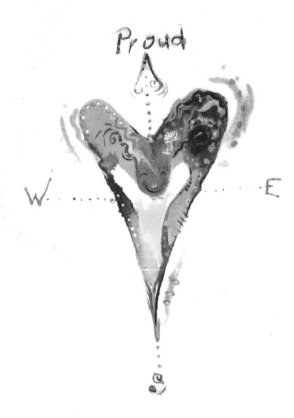

W .... E

S